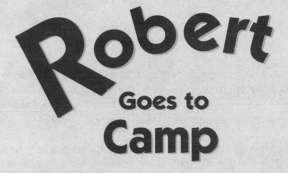

Robert
Goes to
Camp

by Barbara Seuling
Illustrated by Paul Brewer

A
LITTLE APPLE
PAPERBACK

SCHOLASTIC INC.

New York   Toronto   London   Auckland   Sydney
Mexico City   New Delhi   Hong Kong   Buenos Aires

ISBN 0-439-58752-2

All rights reserved. Published by Scholastic Inc., 557 Broadway, New York, NY 10012, by arrangement with Carus Publishing Company. SCHOLASTIC and associated logos are trademarks and/or registered trademarks of Scholastic Inc.

12 11 10 9 8 7 6 5 4 3 2 1   5 6 7 8 9 10/0

Printed in the U.S.A.   40
First Scholastic printing, November 2005

This book is for
Linsey Ilana and Brandon
—B. S.

For Carleton, Kenny and Kevin Krull
—P. B.

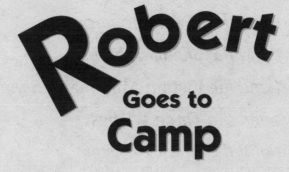

Robert
Goes to
Camp

Also by Barbara Seuling

Contents

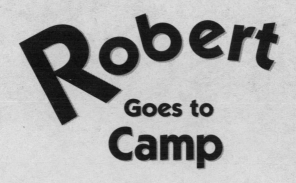

Camp Chickpea

"**C**amp? Why do I have to go to camp?" Robert poked his fork into a mound of green stuff.

"Because," said his mother, "it will be something for you to do during the day while I'm at work. It's just day camp, Robert. Right here in River Edge. You come home at five o'clock. Don't play with your creamed spinach. Eat it."

Robert lifted his fork with some of the green stuff on it. It looked like green slime. He put it down again.

"Dad, you're home in the summertime." Robert's dad was a teacher, with the summer off.

"Yes, Tiger, I am, and I'll be working part-time as a math tutor for Maywood Hills' summer program." Maywood Hills was a couple of towns away.

Robert's dad taught math in high school. He was in a club with other math nuts and wrote papers about math just for fun. Robert never could understand why anyone actually liked math. Now, just when his dad had a whole summer off, he was taking a job as a math tutor. It was too weird.

"I'll be able to drive you to the camp and pick you up. I just won't have time to spend with you during the day."

"Can't I just stay home and play with Huckleberry?" Robert asked hopefully. The big yellow dog lay in the corner of the dining room as they ate. He thumped his tail on the floor when he heard his name.

"You'll like Camp Chicopee, Rob, you'll see," said his mom, pouring iced tea. *Clink, clink, clink* went the ice cubes as they hit the glass.

"Why is it called Camp Chickpea?"

His brother, Charlie, nearly choked on a mouthful of meat loaf. "That's pretty good, Rob," he said, red in the face, laughing.

"It's Chic-O-pee, Rob," said his mom. "It's a Native American name."

Well, at least it wasn't a camp run by people who ate health food, like chickpeas and that stuff called tofu. His friend Paul always called it "toe food," because it probably tasted that bad.

Across the table, Charlie grinned as he continued to wolf down his food. He was thirteen, and ate like he'd never get enough. Robert's mom said all teenage boys ate like that. Robert had never seen anyone with a bigger appetite than Charlie's.

"Charlie is going to Camp Chicopee, too," Robert's mom continued, as though that made a difference. "He's a junior counselor."

Oh, great. That gave Robert one more reason to hate the idea. Charlie was only interested in sports, food, and girls, and all he liked to do with Robert was tease him.

"I loved camp when I was your age," said Robert's dad. A goofy look came over his face. "I learned how to survive in the wilderness like a Native American." He speared a piece of meat loaf with his fork.

There wasn't much wilderness around

River Edge, New Jersey. There were parks with trees and ponds and walking paths. There were ice-cream vendors and picnic benches and restrooms. Robert slid off his chair.

"May I be excused? I want to go over to Paul's."

His mother sighed. "Yes, you may. Be back before it gets dark."

Robert was out the door before he had to listen to one more word about camp.

He ran the three blocks to Paul's house. Paul Felcher had been Robert's best friend since second grade. They had planned on doing a lot of things together this summer.

Robert turned in at Oak Street and ran up the walk. He rang the bell. Paul's mom answered the door.

"Hello, Robert," said Mrs. Felcher.

"Hi, Mrs. Felcher. Is Paul home?"

"Sure. Upstairs, in his room."

Robert ran up the stairs and into Paul's room. Drawings covered the walls. Paul was the best artist Robert knew.

Paul looked up from his computer.

"Hey," he said. "What's up?"

"Hi. Remember that day camp Mrs. Bernthal told us about?"

"Yeah."

"Well, my parents want me to go. I guess it would be okay if we both go. What do you think?"

"I can't," said Paul. "We're going to Vermont."

"Oh," said Robert. He had forgotten that Paul's mom and dad had recently bought a vacation house there. Robert had even been to Vermont with them last winter. "That's so far away."

"Yeah," said Paul. "About five hours in the car."

There was a pause.

"You can grow a beard in five hours," said Robert.

"You can go to China and back in five hours," Paul answered.

"You can learn to play the piano in five hours," Robert continued.

"You can read all the Weird & Wacky Facts books in five hours," Paul added.

They laughed as they went on with each bit of nonsense, and then stopped.

"Maybe you could visit," said Paul.

Robert could do that. His parents would probably say it was all right for him to go for a week or two. But he wasn't sure he could leave Huck. And even if he could go, what would he do with the rest of the summer?

"Yeah, thanks," he said. "That would be great." Robert's shoulders slumped. "I guess we won't be able to do our snake farm this summer." They had talked about getting a couple of snakes with their birthday money, and raising and selling their offspring.

"And our bicycle marathon," added Paul. They had planned on riding as many miles as it took to get to California. Then maybe when they were old enough, they could really do it.

"We can e-mail," said Robert.

"Um, I'm not bringing my computer," Paul said, looking as miserable now as Robert felt. "My parents want me to spend more time outdoors."

Robert noticed some drawings stuffed in Paul's wastebasket. "Are you throwing those away?" he asked.

"Yeah. They're no good."

"They are so!" cried Robert. He pulled out a drawing of a spaceship arriving at an asteroid. Robert wished he could draw even a tiny bit as good as Paul. "Can I have this one?" he asked.

"Sure," said Paul.

"Thanks!"

Robert knew just where he would hang it, on the wall over his bed. He rolled it up carefully.

"I'll write you a postcard," said Paul. "And you write to me, okay?"

"Okay."

On the way home, Robert thought

about the summer. Without Paul around, it wouldn't be much fun to stay home. Riding his bike alone was boring. Huck was great, but he liked to sleep a lot during the day. At least at day camp he'd be with other kids. He heard they went on trips. Joey Rizzo said last summer they went to the Liberty Science Museum, where he got to hold a millipede in his hand. It was as big as a hot dog, with a thousand legs.

Maybe day camp wouldn't be so bad.

Losing Lester

Robert got out of the car, dragging his backpack. A long, low building sat in front of him.

"Well, Tiger, this doesn't look too bad," said his dad. "You're almost in the country here."

A banner over the door of the building read WELCOME TO CAMP CHICOPEE. Behind the building was a wooded area, and no sign of a swimming pool. Robert felt his shoulders relax.

Robert searched the small crowd of campers and parents, looking for someone he knew. He spotted Vanessa Nicolini and waved hi to her. Vanessa had sat next to him in Mrs. Bernthal's class. She always giggled when she spoke to him. Robert never understood why. Vanessa waved back and smiled. He looked for other familiar faces. He wasn't used to doing anything important without Paul.

Just then, an old blue pickup truck drove up. On the door was printed WILLIS RUBBISH REMOVAL in faded letters. It was the truck that belonged to Lester Willis's dad. Lester's dad was in the trash business.

"Yo, Robert!" someone called, jumping down from the pickup.

Just as he suspected. It was Lester's unmistakable voice.

"This your first time here?" he called to Robert.

"Yeah," said Robert. "You've been here before?"

"Last year," said Lester.

Lester was in Mrs. Bernthal's class, too. He used to pick fights with Robert, but things had changed when they discovered they both had trouble with reading. They weren't exactly friends, but Lester was okay, just too big and too pushy.

"Welcome to Camp Chicopee," a man's voice barked over a loudspeaker. Everyone turned toward the voice. At the center of the crowd was a young man with orange hair. Robert and his dad gathered around him with the other kids and their parents. Lester was by himself. Robert hadn't even noticed the blue pickup leaving.

As he got closer, Robert saw that the young man with orange hair was wearing a dark green T-shirt with CAMP CHICOPEE printed on it. He carried a clipboard. "I'm

Dave, the camp director," he announced. "Once I check your name off my list, go over to the counselor with your age group."

"Hello," said Robert's dad when it was their turn. "This is my son, Robert Dorfman."

Dave looked down the list of names on his clipboard. "Yup. He's right here." Dave's arm muscles bulged as he checked off Robert's name. "You're in the Eights and Nines, Robert. Molly is your counselor, over there."

Robert looked where Dave had pointed. A pretty teenage girl with short blond hair held up a sign with 8's & 9's printed on it. A silver whistle hung on a cord around the girl's neck.

"Guess it's time for me to go, Tiger," said Robert's dad.

"Uh, okay, Dad." Robert waved goodbye as he ran toward his group.

"See you at five o'clock," his dad called after him.

Molly wore a Camp Chicopee T-shirt, too, with khaki shorts and sneakers. She smiled at Robert as he walked up to the group. He liked her right away.

Molly grabbed the silver whistle that hung around her neck and blew one loud blast. "Eights and Nines over here!" she shouted, waving a suntanned arm high above her head.

Lester and Vanessa were the only ones Robert knew in the group of about a dozen kids. He recognized some of the others from school, but he didn't know them.

"We'll be spending a lot of time together at Camp Chicopee," Molly said. Lester let out a whoop.

"I'm glad you approve," said Molly, laughing. "When you hear this whistle" — she blew one loud blast—"stop whatever

you're doing and listen. If you have any problems, I'm the one to talk to. Stick close to me at all times," she continued. "We're going to have lots of fun."

Molly explained the rest of the rules and showed the Eights and Nines around the camp.

"One more thing," said Molly. "We get to go on a really cool trip, if you behave."

"Where to?" cried Lester, who always shouted things out.

"It's supposed to be a secret," Molly said, putting her finger to her lips and whispering. "But a little bird told me we're going to South Street Seaport!"

Robert almost shouted "Hurray!" but stopped himself in time.

"Now, you lucky ducks," Molly continued, "grab your things. It's eighty-three degrees today, and that means we're going swimming!"

The other kids cheered, but Robert was dead quiet. There was a pool, after all.

Molly blew the whistle again, and Robert and the other campers followed her to the minibus. Dave was at the wheel.

Lester was close behind Robert as they climbed aboard. Robert looked around the bus quickly. A boy he didn't know sat in the second row, next to the window. Quickly, Robert slid into the empty seat next to him. Lester kept moving toward the back.

Robert wasn't sure why he did that. Maybe he was still uncomfortable around Lester. Lester did everything with so much noise.

"I'm Zach," said the boy next to him.

"Hi," said Robert, putting his backpack down. "I'm Robert."

"Want to hear a good joke?"

"Sure." Robert loved jokes. He and Paul loved telling them. Besides, it would keep him from thinking about the pool.

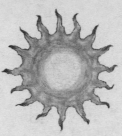

80-Degree Days

"**W**hy was the dinosaur afraid to go back to the library?" Zach asked.

"I don't know. Why?" Robert waited for the punch line.

"Because its books were sixty million years overdue."

Robert laughed, and Zach did, too.

In no time, the bus arrived at the River Edge Community Center, and the campers piled out. Zach explained that any day the temperature reached eighty degrees or higher was a pool day.

Molly took them to a small wooden building. "This is the bathhouse. There are dressing rooms inside, and showers. Boys go over there," she said, pointing to one side, "and girls over there." She pointed to the other side. "When you're in your swim-suits, leave your things on the hooks on the wall and go through the shower. Then meet me here. You have five minutes." Everyone ran for the dressing rooms.

Robert had never undressed in front of other guys before. He followed Zach. If it looked like he and Zach were buddies, Lester might leave him alone.

It didn't take Zach long. "Come on," he said, dashing through the shower. Robert went through after him, more slowly. Zach laughed. "What's wrong? You afraid of water?" Robert felt his cheeks flush.

"No, it's just cold," he replied quickly.

Molly blew her whistle. Robert was glad to move on. As she walked them toward the pool, Molly told them the rules.

"The numbers on the side of the pool tell you how deep the water is. Stay where the water is no higher than your chest. Try to stay with the other Eights and Nines. No dunking. No splashing. No fighting. When you hear my whistle, freeze and listen to what I say." She stopped at the edge of the pool. "Okay, you can go. Last one in is a rotten egg!"

Kids jumped in feetfirst, headfirst, all different ways. Only one or two used the ladder at the shallow end. Robert stood by the ladder, one hand gripping the bar.

Next to him, Zach put on a pair of goggles and cried, "Watch this!" He jumped into the water and swam toward a cluster of girls, splashing wildly.

"Hey!" yelled one of them, jumping out of the way. They all looked annoyed.

"Robert? Aren't you going in?" asked Molly, coming up beside him. Robert was afraid she would call him the rotten egg, but she didn't. She just smiled.

"Uh, sure," Robert answered. He went down one step, gripping the ladder with both hands.

Zach swam back to Robert. "Want to try them?" he offered, slipping off the goggles. Robert slipped slowly down the next step and into the water. He reached for the goggles with one hand as he held on with the other.

"They're really great underwater," said Zach.

Molly smiled and left.

Robert didn't even like getting his hair wet. He couldn't see how goggles could help you breathe underwater.

Before Robert could put on the goggles, a big splash at the deep end of the pool caught their attention. Up through the waves under the diving board a head appeared. It was Lester Willis's head, with his familiar buzz cut.

Lester blew water from his mouth, looking like a sperm whale.

"Lester! Get out of the deep water right now!" Molly called.

"But I can swim!" he shouted back. "And I know how to dive."

"Jump is more like it," said Molly, laughing. "Okay. Move away from the diving area to get out of the next diver's way," she called back. Lester swam to the side of the pool, splashing like a hooked fish. You had to say this for Lester: He sure had a lot of fun in the water.

Why did Lester always have to call attention to himself? Robert bounced up and down in the water on his tiptoes. He tried to keep his upper half dry.

Lester swam over and grabbed onto the ladder. "Yo, Rob," he said. "Isn't this great?" His grin showed all his teeth. Lester climbed out of the water. His swim trunks hung low around his pudgy middle as water poured down around him.

With a soggy *slap, slap* of his bare feet, Lester ran back to the diving board and climbed the ladder. Robert watched as Lester held his nose, took a flying leap, and jumped into the water, sending up a splash that could have drowned the town of River Edge.

Zach looked at Robert. "Are you guys friends?"

"No, not really," said Robert. He felt a little stab of guilt. "Why?"

"I don't know. He's such a jerk. Aren't you going to try the goggles?" Zach waited for Robert to put them on.

Robert tried the goggles on and looked around. Everything was green. He took them off again.

"What's wrong?" asked Zach.

"I can't get my head wet," he said, feeling a rush of guilt for telling a lie. "I . . . I have a hair disease."

"You *what*?"

"I have a hair disease," Robert repeated. "My hair falls out if it gets wet." He quickly handed the goggles to Zach. "Thanks. They're really great." He climbed out of the pool.

"Wait!" Zach called, climbing out after him.

"You don't have to get out," said Robert.

"That's okay," said Zach. "Besides, I have something to show you," he said. "You'll love it." He motioned for Robert to follow him.

Zach led Robert to the back of the bathhouse. He climbed around some bushes. "Look," he said, pointing to a small knothole in the wooden wall of the building.

Robert leaned over and peeked through the hole. A couple of girls walked by with just towels around their middles. Robert jumped back.

"Hey!" he cried. "That's the girls' changing room!"

"Isn't that cool?" said Zach, laughing. "My brother and I found this last year." He leaned over and took a look himself.

Robert tried to be cool, but his skin started to itch.

"What's the matter?" asked Zach.

"Nothing. I . . ."

Molly's whistle blew.

"I wonder what she'd do without that whistle," said Zach.

"Yeah, I wonder," said Robert, relieved to hear it blow. He left the bathhouse and walked quickly in Molly's direction. Zach had to run to keep up.

Panic!

It was time to go. Molly got everyone out of the pool. As they walked to the bath-house, a small green snake slithered by in the grass.

"Look!" cried Robert.

"EEEEK!" cried one of the girls, jumping out of its way. The snake hurried to a rock and froze there.

Robert bent over to look closely at the snake. Zach looked over his shoulder.

"It's just a garden snake," Robert said. "Isn't it beautiful?" He reached down quickly and picked it up for Zach to see.

"You like snakes?" Zach asked.

"Yeah," said Robert. He had liked snakes ever since Mrs. Bernthal bought Sally, a pet snake, for their classroom. Snakes had nice markings and little red tongues that darted in and out.

"Here. Want to hold it?"

Zach reached out and touched the snake. He smiled. "That's cool! Are you taking it home?"

"No," said Robert. "My mom would kill me."

"Let me have it." Zach held out his hand for the snake.

"Really?" Robert gave it to him. "You'll need a tank for it."

Zach put the snake in his shirt pocket.

They got dressed. Robert was embarrassed, but he bravely took off his swim trunks and changed into his underwear and pants.

They met Molly outside.

"Tomorrow," she said, walking toward the bus, "is Games Day."

"Hurray!" shouted a boy from the Tens and Elevens. "I won the zucchini race last year."

"What's a zucchini race?" Robert asked Zach.

"You start with your arms piled with twelve zucchinis. You can't drop them or you're out. You run zigzag around a dozen pails and drop one zucchini in each pail. The first one back to the starting line wins."

"I like the three-legged race," said another boy. "You tie your leg to someone else's and then run together. It feels like you're a monster with two heads and three legs."

Robert had to admit, it did sound like fun. And it meant no swimming.

On the ride back to camp, Robert and the other boys from the Eights and Nines sat in the back of the bus. The girls were singing loudly up in the front.

"What a lot of noise!" yelled one boy, covering his ears.

"Yeah, quiet up there!" yelled another.

The girls made faces at them and kept on singing.

"Watch this," said Zach, getting up and moving a couple of seats forward, nearer to the girls.

Robert saw Zach reach into his pocket and toss the green snake over the seat where Vanessa was sitting.

"EEEEE-EEEE-EEE! GET IT OFF! GET IT OFF!"

"MAAAAA-AAAAAA-AAAAAA! A snake!"

"HE-E-LP!"

Blood-chilling screams filled the bus as girls flew in every direction.

Zach, meanwhile, ran back to his seat and sat down.

"What did you do that for?" cried Robert.

Before Zach could answer, Dave pulled the bus over to the side of the road. He found the snake and threw it out the door. Molly tried to quiet everybody down. One of the girls was whimpering.

Robert couldn't move. Why did Zach do such a stupid thing? The bus could have crashed. The snake was probably scared and wouldn't find its way home.

A couple of the girls turned around and pointed in his direction. They looked mad. Vanessa was hiccuping.

A shrill whistle sounded as the bus started up again. Molly walked to the back, one hand still holding the whistle. She looked at Robert, then at Zach. "Who did that?" Neither boy said a word. Robert could not tattle.

"Aw, those girls are sissies," said Zach. "It was just a little snake. Robert found it in the grass."

Robert was surprised to hear his name.

"You two stay in your seats until we're back at camp. I'll deal with you later."

Zach snickered as Molly walked away. "Did you see Vanessa jump when the snake landed?" he whispered to Robert.

"I would have jumped, too!" said Robert.

"I thought you weren't afraid of snakes."

"Well, I'm not," said Robert. "But I wouldn't want one thrown at me."

"Yeah," said another boy.

"Me, neither," said a voice from behind. Robert knew it was Lester.

"Oh, come on. It was just a joke. They'll forget all about it. You'll see."

Robert was beginning to wonder about Zach. His idea of fun was sure not the same as Robert's. Even Lester wouldn't throw a snake at anyone. He was pretty sure of that.

"Boy, would I love to get my hands on that whistle of Molly's," said Zach.

Robert didn't answer. He sank down into his seat and wished the bus would move faster.

Back at camp, Molly took the two of them aside. "The snake incident could have had serious consequences," she said. "We're lucky that Dave didn't lose control of the bus. You could have put the other campers in danger. Never do anything like that again. Do you understand?"

They nodded. Robert wanted so badly to tell Molly he had nothing to do with the incident on the bus, but he kept his mouth shut. The last thing he wanted was to be a tattler.

Trouble

The next day, Robert headed for the field where the games were to take place.

Zach was close behind him.

"This is dumb," said Zach, watching Dave handing out pieces of rope for them to tie their legs together for the three-legged race.

"It's fun," said Lester, who was close enough to hear. "Ever try it?"

"No, and I don't want to," said Zach, throwing his rope down and going off to sit it out.

"Want to be my partner?" said Lester.

Robert looked around. All the other kids were already paired up.

"Sure," he said.

Lester tied his right leg to Robert's left leg. They tried walking and fell over in the grass. They got up, laughing so hard they fell down again. Each time they got up and tried to walk, they collapsed in laughter.

As they struggled to get up, Vanessa and another girl tried to run by with their legs tied together. They fell down, too. The girls laughed so hard it got Robert and Lester laughing all over again.

They were laughing so much they almost didn't hear the whistle.

"Everyone, back to the main building," called Dave.

With groans and complaints, Robert and Lester untied themselves and went with the rest of the group back to the main building.

"Okay, settle down," said Dave. "Something is missing, and we need it back."

Surprised faces appeared among the campers.

"What's missing?" called one camper.

"Yeah. We didn't do it," said another. Other campers laughed.

"It's not funny," said Dave. "We don't like dishonesty at Camp Chicopee. Molly's silver whistle is gone."

Robert spun around. Molly stood in the back. The familiar whistle on its leather cord was not around her neck. He looked over at Zach, sitting by himself. Robert remembered that when they were on the bus, Zach said he'd love to get his hands on that whistle—but Zach wouldn't really go ahead and take it, would he?

A couple of boys muttered something low that Robert couldn't hear.

"If the person who took the whistle returns it this morning, we will accept an apology and get on with the camp activities as planned," said Dave. "Until the whistle is returned, you will be confined indoors."

There was a dark cloud over the camp for the rest of the day. The excitement campers had felt about the games was gone. Molly and the other counselors took out board games and crafts supplies, but the mood remained dreary right through lunch and the afternoon.

"No one has returned Molly's whistle," Dave told them shortly before five o'clock. "So all special activities will be canceled from now on, including the trip to South Street Seaport, unless Molly gets her whistle back."

Voices buzzed among the boys. Some voices sounded angry. One of them was

Lester's. "Come on, Zach, 'fess up," he said. "Everyone knows you took it."

The boys' voices got louder. "Yeah, give it back, Zach," said one.

"We're being punished because of you," said another.

Zach looked uncomfortable. He walked over to Dave and held out the whistle, grinning. "It was just a joke."

Dave took the whistle. He looked sternly at Zach. "Taking someone's property is not a joke."

Zach looked like a cornered rabbit. "Well, Robert thought it was okay," he blurted out.

"What?" cried Robert. "I did not!" He felt as though his stomach had been punched, hard.

Dave announced, "Everyone is free to leave, except Zach and Robert." There was a mad rush for the door.

Robert felt like he couldn't breathe.

"I can kick you both out of camp for this," said Dave, when they were alone. "Stealing is a serious offense."

"I didn't steal it," Zach said. "I was just hiding it for a while, as a joke." He fidgeted. "Ask Robert."

Dave frowned. "Robert, what do you know about this?"

Robert opened his mouth. He had heard Zach say he'd like to get his hands on Molly's whistle. So he sort of knew about it. . . .

Suddenly, Charlie burst in. "What's going on?" he asked Dave. "I heard there was a problem with Robert."

"Hi, Charlie. These two are in big trouble. I'm figuring out how they should pay for it."

"What kind of trouble?" Charlie looked at Robert, who was speechless.

"They stole Molly's whistle and were caught."

Robert felt as though he might throw up.

"Wait a second," said Charlie, sitting down. He looked relieved. "No way could this be right," he said. "My brother would never steal anything."

Charlie was sticking up for him! Dave looked uncertain. He turned back to Zach and Robert. Then he looked at Charlie again.

"I don't know," said Dave. "There's something rotten here, but I can't figure out what it is. And I've got to be sure these two deserve to go to South Street Seaport in a couple of weeks."

Robert gulped. This was the trip he had been waiting for.

Dave turned to him and Zach again. "I'll talk to your parents, and you'll have to earn my trust back," he said. "Now go home."

Charlie walked with Robert to the car, where their dad was waiting. Neither of them spoke.

"What's wrong?" Robert's dad asked.

"Robert's in trouble," answered Charlie. "Big time."

Guilt by Association

"So what, exactly, did you do, Rob?" Robert's mom reached into a red-and-white striped paper bucket with a pair of tongs and placed several pieces of fried chicken on a platter. "Do you want to explain?"

Robert swallowed hard. Wow. Dave didn't waste any time. He must have called already. What did he say? That Robert was a thief? He had to show his parents he was not a thief. He told them everything.

Robert told them about taking the seat next to Zach on the bus. He told them about Zach teasing the girls in the pool. He told them about the hole in the girls' dressing room wall. He told them about Zach and the snake.

"I thought he wanted it for a pet," he said. "I didn't know he would toss it at the girls!"

He told them about Zach making it look like Robert had something to do with taking Molly's whistle.

"This Zach," his father said. "How come you hang out with him? He sounds like a bad egg to me."

Why did grown-ups turn everything into an egg? Molly said the last one in the pool was a rotten egg. Now Zach was a bad egg. Robert couldn't say why he was always with Zach. His excuse sounded so dumb: Zach told good jokes. He seemed to like Robert. He made Robert feel like he had a pal at camp.

"It's clear, Robert, you have a situation here," said his father.

"It wasn't my idea to peek through the hole in the wall. I didn't even know what I'd see there."

Charlie laughed with a mouth full of chicken. "I'll bet!" he managed to say.

Charlie was probably right. He should have figured that one out.

"What about the snake? And the whistle? It's not fair. I'm in trouble, and I didn't do anything." He stabbed his mashed potatoes with his fork.

"Well, maybe you did and maybe you didn't," his father said.

"Huh?"

"Tiger, if you hang around with a kid who does stupid things, that makes you seem just as stupid."

"It's called 'guilt by association,'" added his mom.

"You mean, if I associate with someone, and they do something wrong, I'm guilty, too?"

"You got it," said Charlie, pointing his fork at Robert.

Robert slumped in his chair. "Great. So now, for trying to avoid Lester, I'm in trouble."

"Lester? I thought you and Lester were friends."

"No, Mom. Lester's a . . . Well, I helped him with his reading, and we did a couple of projects together, and he eats lunch with Paul and me sometimes, but we're not exactly friends." Robert squirmed. Lester had actually been nice to him quite a bit since the days when he was a bully.

"I see," said his mom, passing the biscuits around. "So does Lester cause any trouble?"

Robert shook his head. Come to think of it, it had been a long time since Lester had actually bothered anybody. "So what do I do now?"

"You have to show Dave he can trust you, Rob," said his mom. "Right now, he's not sure he wants you to go to South Street Seaport."

"You can't blame him," added Robert's dad, picking up a chicken wing with his fingers.

If only Paul were here. Paul would help him prove he was not a thief. Robert twirled his fork as he thought. *If Paul were here, I wouldn't be in trouble in the first place.*

Robert was suddenly angry at Paul for leaving him alone this summer. None of this would have happened if Paul hadn't gone away.

Robert kept playing with his fork while his mom put out fresh strawberries and vanilla ice cream for dessert. It was one of his mom's best desserts, but Robert could not eat any.

That's stupid, he thought as he pushed a strawberry around his bowl. Paul hadn't done anything. Robert had gotten himself into this mess on his own, and he would just have to get out of it on his own.

After the dishes were cleared away, Robert went up to his room. Huckleberry followed him, his toenails *click click click*-ing on the stairs. Robert sat on the floor to scratch Huck behind the ears and hug him. Hanging out with Huck would have

been better than camp. He never got into trouble with Huck. Huck was his pal and never let him down. The big yellow dog rolled over on his back for a belly rub.

Robert put on his headphones and slipped a CD into his Walkman. It was his favorite band, the Sprockets. "Ooo-ooo-ooo, you're nothing but a heartache, nothing but a heartbreak, you-ooo-oooo."

Yeah, his heart ached all right. One thing was for sure: It was easy to get into trouble and a lot harder to get out of it.

He took off his headphones and wandered downstairs. Huck trailed behind him. His dad was watching the news. Robert lay on the floor to watch with him, and Huck flopped down next to him.

The weatherman came on and announced a beautiful day tomorrow. "Not a cloud in the sky," he sang out. "Bright sunshine and ninety degrees. See you all at the beach."

Robert couldn't decide which would be worse—braiding another wristband in crafts or going swimming. He rolled over and buried his face in Huck's soft fur.

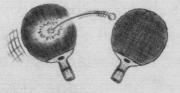

Ping-Pong

Robert had asked his dad to drive him to camp a little early, so he could talk to Dave before the other campers arrived. Charlie usually rode ahead on his bicycle, to get there early for Dave's daily meeting with the counselors, but today he went with them by car.

"I wish I could help you through this, Tiger," said his father. "Just be honest and own up to what you did. It wouldn't hurt, either, to take a good look at your friends."

"Thanks, Dad." His dad thought he was so brave and even called him by the nickname "Tiger." Robert didn't have the heart to tell his dad he felt like a coward. He got out of the car with Charlie and headed for the main building.

Dave was sitting backward on a chair, talking with several counselors as Robert and Charlie walked in.

"Aren't you early, Robert?"

"Yes. I need to talk to you."

"Go ahead."

Robert's mouth was dry.

"Let's go, guys," said Molly, getting up. "We can come back later." She motioned to the other counselors to follow her. Charlie gave Robert a thumbs-up as he left with the others.

"So, what is it?" asked Dave.

"I . . . I'm sorry for the trouble I caused."

The words almost stuck in his throat. He wanted so badly to say "I didn't do anything!" but he knew his dad was right. Hanging out with Zach made him just as responsible.

Dave looked him in the eyes. "Apology accepted. But one more goof-off and you're grounded. Understand?"

"Yes," Robert said.

"Okay, then. Go outside. Your group should be arriving any minute. Tell the counselors to come back in."

"Thanks."

Robert did as he was told. Dave didn't say anything about South Street Seaport. Robert figured he still had to prove he could be trusted.

How did he get into this mess? He was never in trouble before. Zach, that's how. Robert saw Zach arrive and walked in the opposite direction before Zach could spot him.

On the bus to the pool, he passed Zach and sat next to a boy he didn't know, farther back. Suddenly, Robert saw that it was his own fault. If he had been nicer to Lester, none of this would have happened.

It wasn't bad at the pool. While the other kids splashed in the water, Robert wandered over to watch some Ping-Pong. Both tables were in use. Robert watched a game between a girl and a boy.

The girl really knew how to play. She was fast and smart. She knew how to surprise the boy with sudden moves. She got points several times for slamming the ball so he couldn't hit it back. The boy left after the game. He had lost, twenty-one to six.

"Want to play?" asked the girl. Robert looked around. There were no other kids waiting to play. Did she scare them all away?

"No, I'm only just learning."

"Play me. Come on."

Robert came closer, but he hesitated to pick up a paddle.

"I'm Andrea. What's your name?"

"Robert."

"Well, Robert. Pick up a paddle, and I'll show you a few tricks."

Robert picked up the paddle.

"You serve." Andrea bounced the ball across the table to him.

Andrea didn't play as hard and as fast with Robert as she had with the other boy. He was glad. He liked Ping-Pong but he couldn't keep up with a fast game like that.

"Aren't you the kid who got in trouble?"

Uh-oh. She knew! "Yes," he said.

"You don't seem like a troublemaker."

"I'm not," he said. Now he sounded like a wimp.

"Good." Andrea slammed the ball and won the game. Robert never even saw it coming.

"Sorry," said Andrea, "I couldn't help it. You practically asked for it. You have to pay attention to the ball and what the other person is doing. Keep the ball low, near the net, so that the other person can't slam it."

Andrea wasn't bossy. She was just a good player. Robert liked learning from her. They started another game.

"You're not so bad," Andrea said.

Robert returned her serves. That was half the game, Andrea told him. He had a lot more to learn.

The whistle blew. It was Molly's whistle. "That's my group," said Robert. "I have to go."

"Okay, see you." Andrea waved a paddle at him. "We'll play again next time. You're getting good."

"Thanks," said Robert, waving back. It was so nice to feel good about something for a change.

Andrea wasn't at the Ping-Pong tables the next day, but Robert sat on the grass and watched some games.

Vanessa came by. "You playing or watching?" she asked.

"Um, watching, for now," he answered. He was embarrassed that he still hadn't figured out a way to apologize to Molly and the girls.

"Me, too," said Vanessa, sitting down next to him.

Robert was dying to play. He felt he was getting better at his serve. But he was too shy to play in front of Vanessa.

After that, Vanessa came by each day and sat on the grass, watching one game after another.

One afternoon, Dave called Robert over. Molly stood nearby.

"Molly and your brother Charlie put in a good word for you," said Dave. "I trust them, so I'm giving you a chance. You can go to South Street Seaport." He glared at Robert. *"Don't disappoint us."*

"I won't!" Robert cried, taking a flying leap at Molly to thank her and almost knocking her over.

"Whoooooo-oooa!" she said, laughing. "Take it easy. I want to get there in one piece!"

Robert ran back to Vanessa, flopped down on the grass, and told her the news. He was so happy that he hardly had a chance to be embarrassed when Vanessa squealed and hugged him.

South Street Seaport

The days dragged on. Robert was used to camp now, and he had managed to avoid Zach as much as possible. But it was really thinking about the trip to South Street Seaport that had kept his spirits up.

At last they were on their way.

Robert noticed that Zach was not with them on the bus. He felt sorry for him, but at the same time, he was glad he didn't have to worry about Zach all day.

The air at South Street Seaport was part salty sea breezes and part the smell of fresh fish from nearby markets. Robert didn't mind. It was exciting to be there.

Anchored in the seaport harbor were several ships. One ship had a tall mast and lots of sails and a red flag with a white cross on it. Sailors were all over the ship, on the deck or climbing the rigging. One called down to them and waved. Robert waved back.

"Hello, Americans!" the sailor shouted. He looked no older than Charlie. Molly explained that the ship was a training ship from Denmark. The Danish Navy trained its young men on all kinds of ships, on voyages to all parts of the world. This one was an old sailing vessel that now had an engine.

Molly took her group of Eights and Nines aboard an American merchant ship from the nineteenth century. Charlie brought his Tens and Elevens on board, too.

Printed signs explained that the sailors did all the work on the ship. They raised and lowered the sails each day. Some climbed the rigging to make repairs. At the very top of the mast was a crow's nest, where a lone sailor could stand in a little basket as a lookout. Robert got dizzy looking up at it.

Robert followed his group down the steps to the lower deck. Charlie and his group were just ahead of them. Charlie and Molly were talking to each other as they moved the campers along.

"Were these for fishing?" Vanessa asked, pointing to a string net hanging between two posts.

"No," said Molly. "Those nets are where the sailors slept."

"They slept in these?" cried Lester.

"Yes," said Molly. "There were no luxuries on a merchant ship."

"Oh, look," said Vanessa. She went inside a tiny room with a bunk in it.

"That's where the captain slept," said Molly, reading a sign on the cabin door.

They passed long tables and benches bolted to the floor. "This is the galley," said Molly. "That's what they call the kitchen on a boat." There was a huge iron wood-stove, where the cook made meals for all the sailors, and a pantry, where food supplies were kept in barrels. Everything had to be nailed down or placed in containers so it wouldn't slide when the ship was tossed around, pounded by big waves.

Robert felt the slight rock of the ship on the water but couldn't imagine what it must be like in a storm at sea. How could anyone eat?

As they left the ship and walked past

the ticket booth, Molly pointed to a building across a wide plaza. "We're going into that building," she said. "You can buy something to eat or souvenirs. Stay with your group. If you get separated from the group, meet us back here at the ticket booth in one hour."

The kids went into the building. There were shops and food stands with everything from Chinese food and hot dogs to pizza and burritos. It all smelled wonderful.

Robert stopped at a shop window decorated with fishnets and lobster traps. A tiny sailing ship caught his eye. It looked just like the one they had just been on. The price tag read $5.95. Robert wanted to buy it for Molly. He checked his cash. Ten dollars. He had enough for the ship with four dollars left over. He asked Molly if he could go in.

"Sure," she said. "Meet us up ahead by the food stalls."

"Okay." Robert went into the shop.

Inside, the cashier took the little ship, wrapped it in pink tissue paper, and put it in a box. Robert had forgotten about tax. It came to $6.46.

That left only $3.54 for lunch. He was hungry. His mouth watered as the smells of the various food stands reached his nose. Tacos. Burgers. Fries. Pizza.

A candy shop had a display of giant bags of caramel popcorn, tied with yellow bows. Robert stopped. He could get that for the girls. It would make an apology easier.

The sign under the bags read $2.79. Robert counted his money again. If he got the caramel popcorn, he wouldn't have enough left for a postcard for Paul or even a candy bar for himself. His stomach felt so empty, and they still had a long ride back to camp!

He bought the popcorn. He could write a letter to Paul instead of a postcard.

When they returned to their bus for the ride home, Robert walked over to Vanessa and held out the bag to her. "Here, Vanessa," he said, his voice cracking a little. "I'm sorry for what happened with the snake. This is for you and the other girls."

"Thank you," said Vanessa, staring at Robert. She didn't giggle.

"Ooooh, yum!" said one of the girls with her, coming closer.

Robert's neck started to itch. "I . . . I got to go. See you."

He ran back to Molly. He pulled the box out of his pocket and handed it to her.

"For me?" Molly said. "What is it?"

"Open it." She did, and took out the

pink tissue paper. She unwrapped the little ship.

"Oh, Robert," she said. "This is so sweet!"

"It's just like the ship we were on," he
said.

"I love it, Robert. I'll treasure it.

Thanks!" She leaned over and kissed him on his forehead. He felt his cheeks get hot.

In the background, the other girls stood next to Vanessa, who was holding the big bag of popcorn in her arms, and pointed at him. This apologizing was tough. Not only was it hard and expensive. It was also embarrassing.

Not Again, Robert!

After three eighty-degree days in a row, they finally had a day when they didn't have to go to the pool. Robert was determined to make it a good day. He took out the "Find-a-Tree" paper that Molly had handed out to each of them with a pencil. "See how many different kinds of trees you can identify," she said, as they started out on a nature walk.

The wood behind the camp was not too thick, but it was quiet. A path wound through. Molly was just up ahead. Robert stopped by a tree with star-shaped leaves. He looked down the list. There was a picture of a leaf with the same points. He put a check by "maple."

They walked a little farther, and Robert saw a tree with white bark and leaves shaped like hearts. Looking at his list, he checked off "birch."

Something peeked out from behind a bush. It looked like a cat. It came out. It was not a cat. Robert saw a white stripe on its back. This was a skunk! He stayed very still. He had seen a TV program about skunks once. If you didn't bother a skunk, it would just go away. Otherwise . . .

There was a crunching of twigs nearby.

"Yo, Rob!" Lester jumped out from behind a tree. The frightened skunk lifted its tail and sprayed.

"OOOOOOOOOO-WEEEEEEEEEE!" yelled Robert. He turned his head away but most of him still got doused.

"Yikes!" cried Lester, as the spray reached him, too. The skunk ran away.

Robert could not speak. The smell was so strong it made his eyes water. Molly came running, the other campers following behind her.

"What happened to . . . OH NO!" shouted Molly, making a face and backing away.

"Phew!" cried somebody. "What did you step in?"

"It's worse than that," said another.

"Not again, Robert!" cried Vanessa. Robert winced. Vanessa must be remembering that once, in Miss Valentine's art room, he had left a dead fish from one of their projects in the supply cabinet by mistake. The fish had rotted there over the long Thanksgiving weekend, so by Monday the room smelled pretty bad. Not as bad as this, though—not nearly this bad!

"Everyone, back to camp," said Molly. "I'll meet you there. And try to find some tomato juice!"

Nobody objected. "Let's get out of here," said Zach. "Those guys STINK!" The rest of the campers followed him.

"Take off as many things as you can," said Molly. She held her nose.

Lester pulled off his shirt and dropped

it on the ground. Robert did the same.

"You'd better get rid of those pants, too," said Molly. "And your sneakers."

"Our pants? Do we have to?" said Robert. He knew the answer. The smell was powerful.

"I'm afraid so," said Molly. "It's real hard to get skunk smell out. Tomato juice is supposed to help, if we can find some, but I don't think your clothes will ever be the same. We may have to bury them later. Leave your underwear on. Then run for the showers. Quick!"

Robert took off his pants. Lester did the same. In just their underwear, they ran as fast as they could. Molly was right behind them. As they passed the rest of the group, everyone screamed and jumped out of their way.

Molly found a couple of scrub brushes and powdered soap. "There's no tomato juice here," she said, "so Dave went to get some. Meanwhile, take these things, get in the shower, and start scrubbing. And take off your underwear, too."

There was no choice. They did as they were told. At least Molly stayed outside.

Robert scrubbed. "Hey, Lester, I still stink. Do you?"

"Yes! What do we do now?"

"I don't know."

Just then, Molly shouted, "How are you guys doing?" Was Molly going to walk in on them while they were in the shower?

"We're fine!" Robert shouted back.

"I'll find some clothes for you. Keep scrubbing. I'll be back."

"I think I scrubbed my skin off," said Lester.

"Me, too," said Robert. The sound of brushing and the shower running was all they heard for a while.

Molly came back again. "There are two huge jars of tomato juice right outside the door," she said. "Use a whole bottle each. Pour it on and wash everywhere with it."

"With tomato juice?" said Robert.

"I hate tomato juice," said Lester.

"Never mind," said Molly. "It's not for drinking."

Robert went out to get the tomato juice. "Now what?" he asked, taking the cap off a jar.

"This, I guess," said Lester, as he took the jar from him and poured tomato juice over Robert's head.

"Hey, cut it out!" Robert sputtered. He opened the other jar and poured juice over Lester's buzz cut.

Roaring with laughter now, they were spitting tomato juice while they washed. When they were done, they rinsed off and came out of the showers.

They found towels and clothes neatly stacked on a bench. Next to them was a plastic shopping bag.

The clothes must belong to workmen. They were extra big and full of paint and holes. Robert looked at Lester.

"You look like a clown!"

Lester danced around, making faces. "And you look like a bum!"

They both broke up.

Robert poked a finger through the hole in the knee of his baggy pants. They exploded with laughter. This was almost as funny as the three-legged race.

Lester spilled out the plastic bag. There was baby powder, minty mouthwash, Lady Lilac cologne, bubble gum–flavored toothpaste, deodorant, hair mousse, insect repellent, and sunblock.

"It looks like everyone threw in whatever they had that smelled good," Lester said. He sniffed and made a face. "I guess we can use some."

They tried a little of everything. Robert even rubbed some of the toothpaste on his teeth and rinsed. Nothing they did really covered the skunk smell completely, but they smelled much better.

Outside, Robert and Lester walked back to the main building, the perfume-and-skunk smell still pretty strong around them.

All the kids ran in the other direction, even Vanessa.

They passed a Ping-Pong table.

"Hey! Want to play?" Robert asked. "I can show you something I learned from a really good player." He picked up a paddle.

"Good thinking, Rob," said Lester. "We'll have it all to ourselves. I don't think anyone will want to play with us today."

"Yeah, right," said Robert, laughing.

They played Ping-Pong all afternoon. Nobody bothered them.

Watch Your Back!

Friday night was always pizza and movies at Robert's house. Robert's parents had worked all week and were ready to relax. They let Charlie pick the first movie, *Crouching Tiger, Hidden Dragon,* and Robert chose the second, *Shrek.* He had seen it about ten times already and still loved it. Huck, his tail thumping the floor, stuck close to the pizza box, awaiting his share of the pie.

The phone rang while the first movie was on. Robert didn't mind missing a few minutes of the weird special effects, so he got up to answer. It was Lester.

"Lester?" Robert was truly surprised. "What's up?"

"Hey, Rob," Lester said. "I'm sorry for what happened today."

"Oh, that's okay. You were just clowning."

"No, I wasn't."

"So . . . what were you doing?"

"Trying to warn you."

"Warn me? About what?"

"I heard Zach bragging to some of the kids that he's going to get even with you."

"Get even?" said Robert, feeling his stomach tighten. "For what?"

"He's ticked off that you went to South Street Seaport and he didn't."

"That's not my fault!"

"I know."

Robert tried to sound fearless. He hoped Lester couldn't tell he was trembling. "So what is he planning to do?"

"I don't know," said Lester. "Just be prepared, you know?"

"How can I be prepared if I don't know what to be prepared for?"

"Yeah." Lester sounded like he really felt bad. "Keep your eyes open and watch your back."

"Okay, Lester. Thanks."

"Sure. Oh . . . ," said Lester, "we're going to the lake for a picnic tomorrow. My mom says maybe I'll get the rest of this smell off in the lake. She says you can come if you want to."

A picnic with Lester's family? Hmmm. Maybe that would be a good change. "That sounds neat," he said. "I'll ask my mother. I have a feeling if I stay home she'll make me stay in the bathtub."

"Yeah, this will be a lot more fun."

"Hold on," said Robert.

Robert's mom didn't seem to mind missing some of the movie, either. Robert told her about Lester's invitation. She got on the phone.

"Hello, Lester. Thank you for the very nice invitation. May I speak with your mother, please?"

While his mom talked to Lester's mom, Robert caught snatches of men and objects morphing and twisting into new shapes on the TV screen. Charlie was totally absorbed. After they finished their pizza, Robert lay on the floor, his head resting on Huck's rump, while Huck snoozed away.

A couple of minutes later, his mom came in. "Rob, you have to be ready at ten o'clock tomorrow morning."

Yes! Robert felt better than he had in a long time.

The Willises

The next morning, Robert woke up early. He took a soapy shower and scrubbed himself again. He wore tan shorts over his swimming trunks and his blue T-shirt.

Mr. Willis drove up right on time. His truck had a shell on the back, and kids waved from the windows. "Yo, Rob!" called Lester. "Come on!"

On the doorstep, Robert's mom gasped. "You're not riding in the back of a trash truck!"

"Why not?"

"It probably smells bad. And it's not safe."

"But, Mom . . . I probably smell worse than the truck."

She sniffed. "You have a point there." She started toward the truck. "Good morning," she said to Mr. and Mrs. Willis. They smiled at her from the cab of the truck. Behind them in the cab, on a narrow seat, was a baby strapped into a car seat.

"Pleased to meet you," said Mrs. Willis, holding out her hand. Robert's mom shook it.

"Same here," she said, smiling.

Before she could say anything else, Lester opened the back door of the shell to let Robert climb up. The truck was spotless. It had been transformed from a trash pickup to a family van. Three children were against one side of the truck, sitting on a bench and buckled in. Robert and Lester sat down opposite them and buckled their seat belts.

"Thank you for taking Robert," said his mom. "And have a good time."

Robert gave his mom a little wave as the truck drove off.

The ride was bumpy, but it was great riding in the truck.

"That's Maryann," said Lester, pointing to the biggest girl, about seven. "She's the next oldest, after me."

Next in size was a boy. "This is Jake," said Lester. Jake's front teeth were missing. "And the little one is Grace."

Grace was barefoot. "She won't keep her shoes on," said Maryann, in a bossy kind of voice. She seemed to be in charge of the little kids. When they stopped at a sign, she read off the letters. "S—T—O—P spells STOP," she said.

"S—T—O—P spells STOP," repeated the little ones.

Robert was not used to so many people in one family. It was great. Something was always going on. They played games while they rode. Maryann told them she was thinking of something yellow. The others had to guess what it was.

"Does it have wheels?" asked Lester.

"No."

"A crayon!" said Jake.

"Ask questions first, Jake," said Lester.

"Does it fit in my hand?" said Robert.

Maryann nodded. "Yes!"

Robert guessed it after a few more tries. A banana.

They sang one song after another. Robert joined in.

"We're going for a ride in the car, car,

We're going for a ride in the car, car,
We're going for a ride in the car, car,
Brrrrrrrmmmmmmm, brrrrrrrmmmmmm.
Brrrrrrrmmmmmmm."

At last Mr. Willis drove into a park. A lake sparkled on one side. Mr. Willis parked the truck. A path led to a small beach on the edge of the lake.

"This is our spot," said Maryann. "We always come here."

Robert tried not to show his worry. A picnic and a family outing had sounded like so much fun, he forgot all about going in the water.

The Willises unloaded the truck. Mr. Willis took the cooler. Mrs. Willis took the baby in a plastic baby seat. Lester carried the inner tube. Maryann had the beach bag with the towels. Jake carried a couple of water toys. Grace carried the blanket. Robert carried a straw bag holding an assortment of sunglasses, creams, and toys.

They walked to the small beach and spread out the blanket. Mrs. Willis set the baby seat on it. She unpacked the bags. Mr. Willis opened a small umbrella and attached it to the baby's seat so she would be in the shade.

The little children couldn't wait. They peeled off their clothes and headed for the water.

"Wait!" cried Mrs. Willis. She smeared some sunblock on them, and they were off. Robert watched them splashing and swimming as he took off his shirt. Mrs. Willis insisted on smearing him and Lester with sunblock, too.

"Let's go," called Lester as he jogged down to the water. Robert followed behind, slowly. He watched Lester toss in the inner tube and jump in after it. The smaller kids splashed into the water. There were squeals and splashes all around.

"Come on, Rob," Lester called, pulling Grace into the inner tube and swirling her around in it.

"Me, too!" said Jake, grabbing on to the inner tube as Grace bobbed along.

Robert smiled and waved. "I'm coming," he said, walking slowly into the water. He went in up to his ankles and stopped. He watched Lester steady the inner tube as he took Grace out and let Jake climb in.

Grace sat down in the water next to Robert. He sat down, too, happy to stay right there and go no farther. Grace splashed him a little, and he splashed a little back. She laughed.

"Okay, you're next," he heard Lester

say. Lester, in deeper water, whirled Jake around one more time and let him get out so Maryann could get in. She paddled herself around while the younger children played in the shallow water.

After the children had their turns with the tube, Lester beached it and left them playing in the shallow water so he could swim out to a diving platform in the lake.

"Yo!" he called when he was there and ready to dive off.

The water must be pretty deep out there. Lester was a really good swimmer. Robert felt a pang of jealousy.

The sun was warm on Robert's bare back. The water felt good as it splashed him. The children around him filled cups with water and poured them over each other. He joined in, making them laugh. He couldn't remember ever having fun being in the water before. The morning passed, and he hardly noticed.

"Time for lunch," called Mrs. Willis, opening the cooler. Lester swam in and got the children out of the water. They ran up to the blanket, dripping.

Mrs. Willis handed each one, including Robert, a towel and then a sandwich. It was peanut butter. He wolfed it down, hungry from the ride, the fresh air, the sunshine, and playing in the water. Everyone got a paper cup filled with lemonade from a jug.

They had to wait a half hour before they could go back in the water. That was the rule. Lester plopped down on the sand beside Robert.

"Yo, Robert. What's up? How come you weren't swimming?"

"I . . . can't," said Robert, sifting sand through his fingers.

Lester looked like a fish with his mouth open in a big **O**. "No way," he said. "Don't you swim at the pool?"

"No, I just stand in the water until it's time to come out."

He didn't say how scared he was to be in the water at all. Paul was the only one who knew that. Robert couldn't tell Lester. He already felt like a wimp. He didn't want to make it worse and ruin a great day.

Lester whistled. "You want me to teach you how to swim? I taught Maryann and Jake. Even Gracie is learning."

"Uh, not right now. Maybe some other time." He had to work his way up to the idea.

"Okay. Whenever you're ready, you let me know."

At last it was time to go in the water again. The children shouted happily as they ran back in with their water toys. Mr. and Mrs. Willis went in, too. Mrs. Willis dipped the baby into the water so her legs and back got wet. The baby wiggled and laughed and splashed.

Lester swam out to the deeper water to swim. Robert watched as he worked his way into the water. Maybe he could go a little farther this time. He walked in slowly. When the water was up to his knees, he stopped. What if he went in even farther this time? He took tiny steps until the water was up to his belly button.

He saw Lester's head pop up. The water was probably way over Lester's head out there. The idea of the deep water made Robert's knees buckle. He went back toward shore and played again with Maryann, Jake, and Grace.

At the end of the day, the Willises dropped Robert off at home. The children shouted and waved good-bye to Robert. "Come along anytime, son," called Mrs. Willis from the truck.

Robert's mom waved as she opened the door. "Thank you!" she called. The Willises waved back as they drove off.

"How was it?" asked Robert's mom.

"Great," he said.

"You smell a whole lot better."

Robert sniffed. It was true. He did smell better! Imagine how it would have been if all of him had been in the water!

Up in his room, he found a postcard on his bed. It was from Paul. He recognized the fancy lettering and the colored drawing. He felt bad that he hadn't bought Paul a postcard at South Street Seaport. He flopped down on his bed and held the card up to read:

Dear Robert,
Vermont has lots of woods and lakes. Nick got stung by a bee and I got poison ivy. This is what we look like.
Your pal,
Paul

Robert Dorfman
284 Maplewood street
River Edge, New Jersey
07661

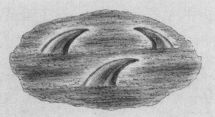

Watch Out for Sharks!

The next week, temperatures climbed into the nineties. Robert managed to avoid the pool by playing a lot of Ping-Pong, or watching others play.

"Hey, Robert, how are you?" It was Andrea. "Come on. Watch me win one," she said. "Then you can play me." Robert liked her confidence.

She won, just as she said she would. Robert played the next game with her. He was faster now and didn't let her slam the ball as often.

"I taught him everything he knows," Andrea joked to those who were watching. Robert blushed, but he felt good having a game with such a good player.

He wished Charlie could see him now! Charlie thought he was hopeless at every sport you could imagine.

Other people were waiting to play the winner, so Robert had to give up the paddle, but at least he got a game in, and didn't do so badly. The score was twenty-one to seventeen.

He passed kids playing Frisbee on the grass. He wandered back to the pool. It was hot, and he could use a soda. The refreshment stand was at the far end of the pool. Lester was clowning in the water, as usual.

The day at the lake had made Robert feel better about the water. Of course, he had only been in up to his waist. Maybe someday . . .

He saw Zach walking in his direction. Robert remembered Lester's warning: *Keep your eyes open and watch your back.*

"Well, look who's here!" said Zach. Robert kept his eyes open. For a moment, the two stopped and stared at each other. Then Zach waved to someone behind Robert and walked on. Just as Robert thought he was clear of Zach, a hard bump knocked him over the edge into the deep end of the pool. "Watch out for sharks!" Robert heard, as he sank below the surface.

Robert thrashed around, holding his breath. He tried to grab at the surface of the water. It was too far away. He felt himself sinking. Pumping his legs and fanning his arms didn't help. He couldn't hold his breath much longer. His ears hurt. He was about to explode!

Something big swept down next to him. He was yanked by his bathing suit. Then up, up he went, until his head was out of the

water. He gasped. He sputtered. Robert felt someone pull him from the pool and lay him on the concrete walk. Coughing, he opened his eyes. Molly leaned over him, her silver whistle dangling over his chest.

He looked over to the side. Lester was hanging on to Zach by the strap of his goggles. Robert coughed and tried to get up. He fell back down, sputtering some more.

Dave ran over. "How is he?" he cried. He leaned over to look at Robert. Robert was beginning to breathe more normally.

"He's okay, Dave," said Molly. "He didn't lose consciousness, so he didn't need CPR. He's got great lungs—held his breath the whole time." Molly held his hand.

"How did it happen?"

Molly pointed to Zach, squirming in Lester's grasp.

"That kid again, huh? Well, I guess we know what to do now." Dave took Zach by the arm. Lester let go.

"Thanks for your help, Lester," said Dave.

"Sure thing," said Lester.

"Thanks, Molly," said Robert. His voice was a little shaky.

"For what?"

"For saving me." He smiled, looking up at her.

"I didn't save you. I sure wish I could say I did."

"Then who did?"

"Lester. He was in the water when you were pushed in. He saw you go down. He dove down, grabbed you, and pulled you up before I knew what had happened. I just helped get you out of the pool."

Robert got up slowly. Lester looked like

a big bowl of pudding with his belly hanging over his dripping shorts. Robert raised
his hand for a high five. Lester responded
with a loud smack of the hand.

"Anytime you want a swimming lesson,
let me know."

Robert couldn't help laughing. "Okay."

Swimming Lessons

"**W**here's my brother?"
It was Charlie, out of breath.

"I heard there was an accident."

"Zach pushed Robert into the pool," Molly explained. "The deep end. But Robert's okay."

Charlie grabbed Robert by his shoulders. "You really okay?" he asked.

Robert nodded. Charlie was probably just showing off for Molly. He turned around. Molly wasn't there.

"You sure?" asked Charlie. Robert nodded. Charlie was really being nice.

"I'm fine," said Robert.

"I have to go back to my group, but come get me if you need me. Okay?" He slapped Robert gently on his back.

"Okay," said Robert as Charlie left.

"Robert?"

He turned toward the familiar voice. "Vanessa! Hi."

"I saw what happened. I hope you're okay." She smiled.

"I'm fine. Thanks."

"That Zach is a pain. He's always bothering someone, but this time, he was plain old mean," said Vanessa. "I know you're not mean like him."

"Thanks." It felt good to hear someone say that. He wished he could say something more, but the words wouldn't come out.

"Here," said Vanessa. She took a braided cord bracelet off her wrist and handed it to Robert. "I made it in crafts."

"Thanks," said Robert. "I . . . like it." He slipped the cord bracelet on his wrist.

Girls were better at saying things. Maybe he could get better with practice.

Molly blew her whistle. "Get dressed!" she called out. "The bus back to camp leaves in five minutes." Everyone ran for the dressing rooms.

Kids boarded the bus, eager to find seats with their buddies. "Yo, Rob," said Charlie, as Robert passed him. "Maybe we can double-date sometime."

Robert's neck itched.

"I was thinking," said Charlie. "I'd better give you swimming lessons. It looks bad for me as a counselor that my little brother can't swim."

Robert smiled. It was the same old Charlie, teasing him, but he had been there when Robert was in trouble. That counted a lot.

"Thanks," said Robert. "I've already got a swimming coach." The seat next to Lester was empty. Robert plopped down in it. "Right, Coach?"

"Really?" Lester asked.

"Really," said Robert. He turned to face Lester. "Hey, do you ride a bike?"

"Yeah," said Lester. "Why?"

Paul would be home in a few weeks. Robert could just imagine them riding their bikes in Van Saun Park like they always did. He could also imagine three bikes, not just two.

"Just wondering," Robert said, leaning back in his seat.

BARBARA SEULING is the author (and sometimes illustrator) of more than fifty books for children, from picture books and freaky fact books to a guide for adults on how to write for children and several chapter books about Robert Dorfman. She divides her time between New York City and Vermont.

PAUL BREWER likes to draw gross, silly situations, which is why he enjoys working on books about Robert so much. He lives in San Diego, California, with his wife and two daughters. He is the author and illustrator of *You Must Be Joking! Lots of Cool Jokes, Plus 17½ Tips for Remembering, Telling, and Making Up Your Own Jokes.*